AF471387

Car Trouble

Domestic Discipline Short Stories

By Jennie May

Car Trouble

Copyright 2009

Jennie May

ISBN 978-0-557-24123-1

Stories

Texting Trouble

Ali pulled out of the gas station and made a right turn. She'd managed to get her errands out of the way quickly and was thankful to be almost home. She reached for the radio to crank up the country music when she heard her phone beep.

She glanced down at her bag and pulled out her sleek, shiny cell phone. It had been a birthday present from her husband. Jim was always up on the latest technology and was sweet about buying her gadgets that would make her life easier.

The message was a text from Jim. It said, "Hey babe. Did you pick up milk?"

She grinned and texted him back, her fingers flying on the tiny keys. "Yes, I did."

She used the texting feature on her phone so often that she'd had to start wearing her fingernails shorter. One of her errands that day had been to stop by the nail salon and get them painted a pretty pink. She loved the way the soft color looked with her long, auburn hair.

The phone beeped again. She pushed the message button as she absently turned a corner. The message said "Are you at home?"

She froze. She knew what he was really asking. When Jim bought her the phone he had laid down the rules. There was to be no talking while driving unless she was using a hands-free device. That rule was easy because Ali liked her little blue-tooth earpiece and because it was illegal to drive and speak on a cell phone at the same time. She knew that they couldn't afford the ticket that would result if she was pulled over. Another of Jim's rules, however, was harder for her to follow. Jim had told her that she was not allowed to text and drive.

She knew that Jim was right. Texting took her eyes off the road and her attention off her driving. It was the instant nature of texting that made her do it, though. She could give an immediate response to a question or statement by just firing off a few letters. It was so quick and easy that she rarely thought about it before responding.

Ali considered her options. She could lie, tell Jim she was still parked at the gas station. She knew she wouldn't do that, though. She just couldn't lie to her husband, and if for some reason he found out she was lying she would be in much bigger trouble than she was already. She decided not to respond at all.

She was only a few blocks from home. As she turned onto their street she could see that Jim's SUV was already parked in the driveway. She pulled her little sedan in beside him and turned off the engine. She grabbed her bags and got out of the car, brushing Jim's big black vehicle as she did. It was warm, which meant he'd only just gotten home himself. She let herself into the house and went to the kitchen to put her groceries away.

He came into the kitchen from the hallway. He had his jacket off, and his tie was loosened. Ali knew he'd been in the process of changing out of his work clothes. He pulled her in for a kiss, and she purred.

Jim was an average height, a few inches taller than his wife. He had dark hair and dark eyes that could smolder with passion when he was aroused or angry. However he was normally very calm and controlled. His personality just didn't lend itself to flying off the handle. He held Ali in his arms and studied her. "You didn't answer my text."

She shrugged a little and smiled. “I was almost home.”

He moved his hands to her waist. “You were driving?”

She sighed, and then she nodded.

He kissed her again. “Are you finished unpacking your groceries?”

“Yes,” she said in a small voice. There had only been a few things to put away.

“Then let’s go talk in the bedroom,” he told her, taking her hand in his.

Ali’s heart thumped. She knew what Jim meant by talk, and it wasn’t talking. Well, maybe Jim would talk for a while. She followed her husband down the hall and into their room.

Jim and Ali had been married two years and had been in their house for only a few months. This was the house where they planned to have a family within the next few years. They were a very traditional couple and had been from the beginning of their relationship. They were both raised in traditional families, and they both wanted their own family to mimic the way they grew up.

In their eyes part of being a traditional couple was that the man was the head of the house, and the woman okpsubmitted both to his directions and his discipline. This was something Ali knew she wanted in a relationship long before she met like-minded Jim.

Jim had been the perfect companion for her. He was steady and easy-going while she had a tendency to get irrational. She brought creativity and spark into his life while he brought order and stability into hers. He was a true leader, always giving her space to express her opinions and giving into her preferences whenever possible. He did not hesitate to correct her, though, especially when he felt that her safety was at risk.

Jim pulled her into their bedroom and sat on the bed's homemade quilt, a wedding gift from Ali's grandmother. He placed his hands on Ali's hips and pulled her toward him, standing her between his parted legs.

"Well?" he asked. "You have anything to say about this?"

Ali took a breath and then shook her head. "I was texting while I was driving. I shouldn't have done it."

Jim nodded. "Okay. But I want to know why you did it. Didn't I tell you it was against the rules?"

Ali sucked on her bottom lip. "Yes."

"And don't you know that it's dangerous?"

She nodded. “Yes.”

Jim shook his head. “Then why?”

Ali thought about it and couldn’t find a reasonable answer. “I just wasn’t thinking,” she finally admitted.

Jim frowned. He appeared to be thinking. “Honey, you need a spanking to help you remember to think before you act.”

Ali wasn’t surprised but she felt herself tremble just the same. She knew he was right. She had disobeyed, and she had to face the consequences. If Jim let these things go, he wouldn’t be the husband she’d wanted.

Jim looked her in the eye, and his voice was stern. “I make rules for your protection. You made a promise to obey when we got married, and I am going to hold you to that promise. Do you understand?”

She swallowed and nodded, forcing herself to meet his eyes. She knew that disobedience was the same as breaking her wedding vows, and that was very serious.

“Driving is a privilege, young lady,” Jim told her. “It’s one that I will take away from you if you can’t handle it responsibly.”

"Please don't," Ali said quietly. She liked the freedom of having her own car and being able to go out when she wanted. She knew that Jim could easily take her car away. She didn't have a job to go to. They'd agreed when they were engaged that she would make their home her focus. She used the car for shopping and other activities. If she didn't have a car, Jim could always take her when he wasn't working.

"I'm not going to do that now," he said. "I do want you to know that it could happen, though. I'm very serious about you driving safely. Let me ask you something. Do you think you would be texting while driving if our children were in the car?"

Ali had never thought about it before, but she knew that once she and Jim had a family she wouldn't take those kinds of risks. She shook her head. "No."

"Why not?"

"Because it wouldn't be safe," she told him.

He nodded. "It's not safe for you either."

"I know," she said softly.

He moved his large hands from her hips and put them around her smaller hands. "This time you're getting a spanking. Do it again and you'll get another spanking and lose your driving privileges for two weeks. Got it?"

"Yes," she answered. Her bottom was tingling already, and her knees were starting to feel a little squishy. Spankings from Jim were nothing to take lightly. He was the kind of man who did everything the best way he knew how, including disciplining his wife. His intention was to make her regret her actions, and he wouldn't stop until he was sure that had happened.

"Go get your paddle," he told her.

She felt a stab of anxiety in her chest, but she obeyed. She opened the top right drawer of her dresser where she kept odds and ends, and she pulled out a small wooden paddle. It was shaped like a stirring spoon, and she knew that it was a lot more dangerous than it looked. She handed it to Jim, and he placed it on the bed. Then he pulled her down across his lap so that her chest and head were supported by the bed but her legs were dangling. Her bottom was centered on his lap. He flipped up her wool skirt and put his hand on her panties.

Ali felt embarrassed, ashamed and anxious. She was already on the verge of tears, knowing she had put herself in this childish position by her own lack of maturity. Jim's hand on her bottom made her feel helpless.

She cringed when he pulled her panties down to reveal her bare bottom. Jim had sometimes spanked her on her panties, and a few times even on the seat of her skirt, but he spanked her bare bottom for serious infractions.

Jim wasted no time. He began spanking her hard and fast, the swats following each other in fractions of a second. She felt the heat immediately, and this was followed by a sting so painful she felt like she had carpet burn. It spread over and into her bottom like olive oil on bread until it saturated her cheeks. The tears spilled and collected on the quilt beneath her, and it wasn't long before she was sobbing.

Jim stopped for a moment and let her get herself under control. "You understand that I'm serious about this?"

"Yes," she cried incredulously. How could she not understand? Her bottom was throbbing.

She felt the paddle tap against her sore bottom, and she sucked in her breath and began to babble through her tears. "Jim, I'm sorry. Please don't paddle me. I'm so sorry."

"Tell me you won't text and drive anymore," Jim said.

“I won’t!” she promised.

Jim brought the paddle down with a loud thwack. Ali jumped and cried out.

“Tell me again,” Jim commanded.

“I won’t text and drive,” Ali shrieked. “I won’t!”

Jim swatted her hard. “Again.”

“I won’t! Jim, I’m sorry! I won’t do it again.”

She felt the next paddle swat low on her bottom cheeks. It hurt. “I won’t text and drive,” she said quickly, squeezing her eyes shut. “I promise.”

He paddled her hard several more times, and she found herself thrust into a storm of tears. When he was finished, he stood her in front of him. She was still crying hard, and her bottom hurt. Her hands flew behind her to try in vain to rub the sting from her sore bottom.

Jim brought her down to sit on his lap, and she flinched as her bottom made contact with his pants. He brushed the hair away from her wet eyes and kissed her on the nose.

“We’re not going to have to do this again, are we?”

She shook her head, although she suspected that sometime over the next fifty or so years she would find herself in this position. She knew that it would most likely be sooner than later. However she knew that the purpose of his question was to confirm that she had learned her lesson about texting while driving, and she had. It was one mistake she was not going to repeat.

She put her arms around him then and rested her head on his shoulder. He held her tightly for several minutes before gently placing her on the bed. "I'll make dinner," he told her.

She smiled up at him and nodded. When he had left the room she allowed herself a few minutes to reflect on this, the marriage she'd dreamed about since she was a child. Then she put her pajamas on and went out to join him for dinner.

Parking Lesson

Charlie Rivers was having a bad morning. He'd woken up at 6am to go for his run but had been stopped by a call from his assistant who informed him that he was having an emergency meeting at 7. Why on earth would anyone have a meeting at 7? Instead of his run, he went straight to the shower. It turned out the meeting was nothing that couldn't have been taken care of a few hours later, and he was annoyed that he had missed the morning exercise that usually kept him energetic and focused throughout the day. After the meeting, he hadn't had time for breakfast because he had three appointments scheduled back-to-back and then was expected to release a response to the huge pile of papers on his desk. Sometimes he found himself wondering if anyone in the city knew how hard their mayor worked on a daily basis.

He had been supposed to have lunch with his wife, Cynthia, but he'd had to cancel. He just had too much to do. Cindy understood.

She always did. Her support of his political career had been something he would always be thankful for. He'd promised her to reschedule for the next day.

At noon, he turned on the television in his office to watch the mid-day news. He liked to be on top of everything happening in the town. The lead story that day was that a new bill was going into effect. Charlie had fought hard to have fines raised on handicapped parking, and it was a change that brought him pride. His mother was in a wheelchair, and his father had heart disease. He knew how difficult it was for them when handicapped spots were taken by the able-bodied who just wanted a better space. The fines in the city had been next to nothing, and people took advantage of that all the time. Charlie was glad that starting that day a much heftier fine would be imposed. The bill even included much stricter consequences if the activity was repeated. In theory a person could go to jail, although he doubted that would actually happen.

Charlie finished watching the news as he read over some new mail that Annie, his assistant, had put on his desk. When the news stories became about weather and then about things like dogs parading around in dresses, he switched the television off. He looked at his watch. He had almost an hour before he had another meeting to attend. If he got enough done, he could go home after that. He would still be working that evening, but at least he could do it from the comfort of his home office while Cindy and the kids chatted in the next room.

He was lost in paperwork when he heard a knock at his office door. “In,” he mumbled.

It was Annie. He knew it would be. Very few people had unrestricted access to his office. She was holding a clipboard onto her chest, her arms folded around it as if it might protect her from something. Her brown eyes were serious. Uh-oh.

Charlie was one of the youngest mayors in the town’s history, a fact repeated as a negative many times by his opponent during the campaign. His good looks and positive attitude were as much a part of his victory as his considerable experience and skills. Annie had been invaluable in helping him promote those assets during his campaign. He had learned to easily read her moods.

“What’s wrong?” he asked her. “Did Janet’s office call again? I’ll take care of it.”

She shook her head. “No sir, it’s something else.”

She paused and appeared tense.

"Well?" he prompted. He was sure it was nothing. Annie tended to get a little worked up about problems that were easily solved.

"It's your wife," Annie said.

Charlie snapped to attention. "Is she okay?"

"She's fine," Annie said. "It's nothing like that." Her heels clicked on the hard floor as she approached his desk. "The news sent this over. They're going to run it tonight at six."

Charlie looked at the small screen Annie had set in front of him. She pushed a button, and a film began to run.

He was looking at a parking lot and the side of a square, white building. It looked familiar.

"It's the library downtown," Annie told him.

He nodded and kept watching. Then his eyes got wide. Then they narrowed. Finally, when the tape ended, he sat back in his chair and looked at his assistant. "They're running this tonight?"

She nodded. "They sent it over in case you have a comment. They're going to ask how the mayor can control the city when he can't control his own family."

"Whoa," Charlie breathed.

“Yeah,” said Annie. “Do you want to see it again?”

“No.” Charlie reached over and pushed a button on his phone. “Rhonda, get Cindy on the phone,” he said sharply.

“Yes sir,” his secretary answered.

He looked at Annie and shrugged. “Thanks.”

She smiled at him. “You want to comment?”

“Maybe later,” he said. “Could you write something up for now?”

“Sure,” she answered. She left the office, shutting the door carefully behind her.

Charlie looked out the window. Today, the day his handicapped parking bill went into action, his wife had gone to the library and parked her car in a handicapped spot. Worse than that, the local news had been filming.

He shut his eyes. Unbelievable.

“Cindy on line one,” Rhonda said through the speaker on his phone.

He picked it up. “Hi, Cin.”

“Hi there,” she answered. “Is something wrong?” He rarely called her at work unless it was to schedule or cancel a lunch.

"What's your schedule like this afternoon?" he asked.

"I can open it up," she told him.

"Good. Come to my office at two."

"Charlie? Why?" she asked him, puzzled.

"Just be here at two, please," he said. He was aware that his voice sounded stern. "See you then?"

"Sure," she answered, her curiosity obvious.

"I love you, Cin," he said.

"Me too," she answered.

Then he hung up and prepared for his meeting.

Cindy arrived at two-thirty. She put her briefcase down by the door and kissed him on the cheek. "Hi babe. Sorry I'm late. I was shuffling some appointments."

"It's no problem," he told her. "Have a seat."

She seated herself in the leather chair opposite his desk and smiled. He noticed for the millionth time how beautiful she was. She was dressed professionally in a gray tailored skirt and jacket with an ivory blouse underneath. Her dark blonde hair curled around her face, showing off her green eyes. He noticed she'd recently freshened her makeup. She leaned forward in the chair. "What's going on, Charlie?"

“The handicapped parking law went into effect today,” he told her.

She smiled. “I know. I’m so proud of you.”

He nodded and folded his hands on his desk. “Did you go to the library today by any chance?”

She looked at him quizzically. “How did you know that? We weren’t having lunch, so instead I knocked out some errands. I had a book to return for Jamie.”

Charlie nodded. Jamie was their seven-year-old daughter.

“Do you happen to remember where you parked?”

She appeared to think for a moment, and then her eyes flew to meet his. “I was only in there for five minutes.”

“Doesn’t matter,” he told her.

Her mouth dropped open. “But how did you know?”

“The news was there, Cindy. They have footage, and they’re showing it at six.”

“Oh shit,” Cindy hissed. She put her perfectly manicured hands to her face.

“Yes,” her husband agreed.

"Charlie, I'm so sorry. I had no idea I was being filmed," she said.

Charlie got up and stepped around his desk. He leaned on the large piece of furniture when he was directly in front of his wife. He crossed his arms and looked down at her.

She began to look nervous. "Are you angry?"

He nodded. "Yes. And it's not about the news team, Cin. What makes you think you can flaunt the laws of this city? Why on earth would you park in a handicapped space? Is something you make a habit of?"

Cindy sighed. "Well… sometimes I just have to duck into a store or someplace else. I need a good parking spot so I can get in and out. You know how busy I am."

Charlie stared at her. "I cannot believe you. Are you telling me this is something you do regularly?"

Cindy blinked. "Not regularly. Just sometimes."

Charlie didn't know what to say. "You know the fine has become very stiff for that particular infraction."

"I'm the mayor's wife," Cindy countered. "No police officer is going to write me a ticket for anything."

Charlie's eyebrows raised. How had this happened? How had he allowed his sweet wife to feel she was entitled to break laws because he was the mayor? This had to stop and the sooner, the better.

"We don't need the police to enforce anything here," he told her. "I'm perfectly capable of enforcing this law myself."

She stared at him. "What do you mean?"

"I'm going to make you see how serious this matter is, and I'm going to impress upon you that you are not entitled to a free pass because you are married to me. In fact, it is your responsibility to be above reproach, young lady."

He saw his wife visibly shiver. It had been years since he'd used those words and that tone with her. It had also been years since he'd last spanked her, but that was about to change.

"Stand up," he ordered.

She stood, and he could see that she was nervous. Even in heels, she was significantly shorter than he was. She looked the part of a professional, but looking down at her with anger in his eyes he saw her more as a little girl dressed as a grown-up.

"Charlie let's talk about this," she began.

He cut her off. “Oh we will talk about this. But first I’m going to spank your bottom to remind you that you are not better than any other citizen in this community.”

She was shocked. “We don’t do that anymore…” she began.

“We do if the situation calls for it,” he said simply. He strode to his office door and locked it. Then he turned back to his wife. “Go stand in the corner.”

Cindy looked as if she might argue but then she did as she was told. He smiled when he saw his professional, all-business wife with her nose in the corner like a naughty child. He pushed his phone. “Rhonda, I’m finished for the day. Why don’t you go on home?”

Rhonda’s voice was pleased. “Thanks,” she said. “See you tomorrow.”

Charlie gave Rhonda plenty of time to get out of the office before he addressed his wife. “Come over here, Cindy.”

Cindy turned and went to stand in front of Charlie. He looked at her for a few minutes and then removed her jacket. She allowed it to fall off her shoulders, revealing the silk blouse. “What you’ve done,” he began. Then he shook his head. “Do you have any idea what you’ve done?”

She shrugged. “I guess not,” she said meekly.

“For one thing, you’ve undermined my authority in this city. What does it say about my leadership if my own wife doesn’t respect the law? They are going to ask that on the news tonight,” he told her.

“I didn’t mean for anyone to see,” she defended herself.

“Cynthia,” he said sharply, “that is not the point. What you did was wrong legally and it was wrong morally.”

He reached for the zipper on her skirt, and she froze. He pulled the fabric off easily and then pushed her panty hose down to her knees. Her silky panties followed. She blushed.

Charlie sat on the edge of his desk and pulled his wife to him. He leaned her across one leg and began to slap her bare bottom with force.

As her bottom turned from a pale white to a ruddy pink, Cindy tried to kick her legs. The panties and panty hose bound them tightly together, and she couldn’t move far. She took a gulp of air and let out a yelp.

“You are not above the law,” he told his wife sternly as he swatted the full cheeks of her bottom. “You are required to follow the law, and there will be consequences if you don’t. Do you understand me?"

"Yes, Charlie," she said in a high voice. He didn't have to look at her face to know that she was crying and that her bottom was getting tender. He reached behind him and pulled a ruler off of his desk He smacked the her thighs, and she nearly jumped off his lap.

"Charlie, no!"

He slapped her bouncing bottom with the ruler again and then again. She was twisting for all she was worth, but he held her in place.

"I don't know where you got the idea that the rules do not apply to you, but you can get it out of your head right now. I will not tolerate disrespect of the laws of this city or of my own personal rules for our family. Do you hear me?"

"Yes!" Cindy responded. "I'm sorry."

He finished with ten quick spanks to his wife's red sit-spot, and when he let her up she was trying to catch her breath.

"You'd better not ever do this again," he said in a tone he hoped conveyed he meant business.

She shook her head. "I won't, Charlie. I won't."

Her mascara was running, and there were streaks down her face from her tears. With a hand on the small of her back, he guided her into the corner again. “You can stand there while I finish my paperwork.”

She was crying harder now, in part because of the humiliation of having to stand bare-bottomed in the corner and in part because her bottom was stinging. He knew she that was especially hard for her, but he wanted to her to understand that he wouldn’t tolerate her behavior.

He watched her cherry red bottom shake as she cried. Then he sat down at his desk.

“I’m going to have to make a statement,” he told her. “What should I say?”

She sniffed. “I don’t know.”

“I think I should say that you were a naughty girl and that you got your hiney spanked.”

Cindy turned from the corner, her eyes huge. “You wouldn’t.”

He smiled. “No, I wouldn’t. Not this time, anyway. Now turn back around before I spank you again.”

Old School Mechanics

The coffee pot on the other side of the room made a gurgling sound. Tia could smell the fragrance of the fresh coffee mixing with the gasoline and motor smells from the next room. Through a large glass window she saw her car. They had it several feet off the ground and were looking underneath. She wondered if all that poking around with wrenches and metal objects was really going to help the situation.

Tia folded her hands in her lap and sighed. If cars had feelings, hers would be pretty angry.

She glanced at the television where a couple of soap opera stars were standing over a hospital bed saying something dramatic. She wondered if anyone would care if she changed the channel. She spotted a remote on the coffee table in front of her, but she changed her mind. She knew there wouldn't be a television program that could distract her from the events of the morning.

She didn't see the man sit down in the chair beside her, but she felt his presence.

"You look like you're waiting to go into the principal's office," he said.

She turned toward the voice. It was Mr. Brand, the mechanic who owned the shop. He was older now, in his sixties she guessed, and seemed to run the front desk and oversee things in the building. Tia knew that his sons worked on the cars.

She smiled at him. "I guess I'm just worried about the car."

"One thing I learned long ago is that a car is just a thing. It's people that really matter, and the main thing is that you're okay," he said, nodding toward her. His kind blue eyes were surrounded with comforting wrinkles, and Tia felt a little better. She knew what he'd said was true.

"Let's just hope my husband agrees," she said with a smile.

"I guarantee you he will," said Mr. Brand.

"I know he'll be thankful I'm safe," she agreed. "But he's still going to be angry."

Mr. Brand's brow furrowed. "Will he now? What happened exactly?"

Tia felt her face turn red. This was such an embarrassing story to have to tell. She might as well practice with Mr. Brand, though, before she had to tell it to Doug.

"Well… well, I was at the intersection of Pine and Route 27. I wanted to make a left, and I really didn't see anyone coming. I dropped my sunglasses case on the floor, and when I went to pick it up, the car just ran right into me."

Mr. Brand nodded. "You were making a left turn while you were picking up your sunglasses case?"

She nodded glumly and absently dug with her shoe at the faded rug beneath her feet.

"So the accident was due to carelessness on your end," Mr. Brand concluded.

Tia nodded again. "Yes. So you see, Doug isn't going to be thrilled."

Mr. Brand rubbed the white stubble on his chin. "I suppose not."

Tia closed her eyes. She didn't know what Doug was going to say, but it wasn't going to be good. She had a fairly good idea what he was going to do, though.

“Doug’s a sensible man,” said Mr. Brand. “I’ve known him for years. He won’t overreact.”

Tia smiled ruefully. “I guess it depends on your definition.”

Mr. Brand eyed her. “Now you’re not scared of your husband, are you?”

She shook her head. “Oh no. Doug would never hurt me, not really. He just… well, he’s old-fashioned.”

“Ah,” said the older man. “Doug wears the pants in the family, eh? That’s unusual this day and age.”

“That’s how we wanted it,” Tia said simply, not sure how much detail she wanted to offer.

“You know,” said Mr. Brand, “my son is about your age. He was married a few months back. I have always taught my boys that women are to be protected, loved and admired. Women are the weaker sex. I know that’s not a popular opinion these days, but I believe it’s true. They have certain emotional needs that men just don’t have. Anyway, I taught my boys that a woman should be treated carefully, like a precious gem. If she needs help to keep herself safe and protected, then it’s her husband’s job to help her do that. He should allow no one to hurt her, not even herself.”

Tia studied the rug. That was very similar to Doug's approach to life and relationships. "I… well, I always wanted a man who would take care of me and kind of keep me in check so I could be myself. You know?"

Mr. Brand nodded. "I do. My boy found a woman who feels the same way you do, and I'm thankful for that. I hope my younger son will find someone traditional as well."

"And what would you tell Doug if he was your son?" Tia let her gaze meet his.

"Honey, I'd tell him to spank your bottom red for being so careless with your own safety," Mr. Brand said. Tia saw both compassion and a flicker of sternness in his eyes.

"I thought so," she said.

"You don't think you deserve a spanking?"

"I know I do," Tia admitted. "That doesn't make it any easier."

"I suppose not," the older man agreed with a smile. "Just remember that you're lucky to have a man like Doug."

"I know I am," Tia said. She meant it. She did love her husband completely, and she wouldn't want him to be any different than he was.

Mr. Brand stood up and gave her shoulder a friendly squeeze. “He’s lucky to have you too.”

Tia hoped that was true. She watched Mr. Brand go back to his desk and then turned when she heard the front door open.

Doug strode into the room. He wore his work shirt and a tie, although he had apparently left his jacket in the car or at the office. He went straight to Tia and pulled her up out of her chair. “Are you okay? Are you hurt?”

She shook her head. “No, no I’m fine. I told you on the phone.”

He put a hand on each of her shoulders and moved her an arm’s length from himself. He looked her over as if he wanted to be sure she was okay.

“You scared me,” he said.

Tia was shocked to see tears in her strong husband’s eyes. “I’m sorry,” she said. Doug pulled her in close and she sighed against his chest, breathing in his scent as she felt his strong chest hold her. When he released her, he continued to hold her hand.

Doug turned to Mr. Brand. “How’s the car?”

The older man looked up from the desk and shook his head. “I don’t think it’s good news,” he said. “I’ll know more in an hour or so.”

Doug nodded and turned back to his wife. “So what happened?”

Tia glanced at Mr. Brand, who smiled gently and with encouragement.

“It was all my fault,” she blurted. “I wasn’t paying attention. I was looking for something on the floor, and the other car ran into me.”

Doug nodded slowly. “I see. And what did the police say?”

Tia’s heart lurched. She stepped over to Mr. Brand’s desk so she could easily see into her handbag. She pulled out several pieces of paper and handed them to her husband.

Doug looked at her hard for a few seconds and then turned his attention to the paper. “One ticket for reckless driving.”

Doug put the ticket on the desk and looked at Tia. “Yes,” she said.

He nodded. “A ticket for not wearing a seatbelt?”

Tia swallowed as Doug put the ticket on top of the previous one. “I had to take it off to reach the sunglasses case.”

“And a ticket for speeding? Tia!” Doug looked shocked.

Tia cringed. “I just wasn’t paying attention.” She looked at Mr. Brand, who was shaking his head.

"You didn't tell me about the speeding, young lady," Mr. Brand scolded.

"So let me get this straight," Doug said, placing the last ticket on top of the others. "You were speeding, not wearing a seatbelt and not looking at the road when this other car hit you?"

Tia nodded. It sounded really bad in those terms.

Mr. Brand looked at Doug. "We won't be able to tell you anything about your car for awhile yet. If you'd like some privacy, I have a back room you could use. It's just a storage room for extra parts and supplies. If you'd be interested in using it, you can be my guest."

Doug nodded. "Yes, we would. Thank you."

"It's down the back hall right across from the restrooms," said Mr. Brand. "It locks from the inside."

Doug pulled Tia firmly by the hand, and she stumbled as she followed him. He lead her down the hall and into a room she had never known was there. She couldn't remember when she'd been so embarrassed. Mr. Brand not only knew that Doug was going to spank her, but he had offered a room.

Just as Mr. Brand had said, the room was filled with boxes of auto parts. Doug clicked the lock, and then he stood to look at his wife.

“Take your pants down,” he ordered, wasting no time.

Tia nervously fumbled with her pants. She pushed them down to her knees and stood in her white panties.

Doug studied the room. He took one large box and placed it on top of another. Together they were just under the height of Tia’s waist. After arranging the boxes, Doug stood in front of Tia.

“Tia Annalisa, I am very disappointed in your behavior,” Doug told her. His face was set into a firm expression that made Tia shaky.

She shifted her weight from one foot to another. “I know,” she said.

“You were irresponsible, and you put yourself in danger,” he told her. Then he titled her chin up so that she was looking into his face. “You put my wife in danger, Tia.”

Tia felt her face grow warm with shame. “I’m sorry.”

Doug nodded and regarded his wife. “I know you’re sorry, and you should be. Now you’re in big trouble. You’re about to get your bottom spanked in a mechanic’s shop.”

A small whimper escaped from Tia’s lips.

“Are you embarrassed that Mr. Brand knows you’re getting a spanking? You should be. You should be embarrassed that you have earned yourself a spanking at all.”

Tia couldn’t look Doug in the eye. She focused instead on one of the boxes on the floor.

“Put your elbows on the box,” Doug told her.

Tia moved toward the boxes and put her elbows on top as Doug had said. She was bent at the waist, and her bottom thrust itself toward her husband.

Doug grabbed her bottom roughly through her panties. “Are you ashamed of yourself, Tia Annalisa?”

“Yes sir,” Tia whispered.

“Speak up,” Doug said sharply.

“Yes sir,” she repeated.

Doug tugged her panties down to her knees, and Tia gasped. It wasn’t that she didn’t expect Doug to bare her bottom. He nearly always did.

Tia steeled herself as her husband grabbed her firmly around the waist and began spanking her bottom hard and fast. Doug’s hands were large, and they were strong. When he flexed them, as he was doing, they felt like a paddle.

It wasn't long before Tia began to wiggle her bottom frantically. Doug ignored the movement and continued his brisk pace. He covered every inch of her bottom.

When the pain got too intense, Tia pushed herself up onto her hands.

"Elbows," Doug commanded sharply, and Tia brought herself back down again.

A few minutes into the spanking Doug increase the force behind each swat. Tia cried out at first and then started kicking her legs.

"Keep those legs still, young lady, or I'll ask Mr. Brand for something to tie you down," Doug warned. He smacked her thighs three times each, and she started to cry.

Doug took this as his cue to begin a lecture. He also slowed the pace of the spanking, but each blow was delivered forcefully and with excruciating accuracy. He aimed for the bottom of her cheeks, which were already tender and sore.

"I'd better not ever catch you driving even one mile over the speed limit," Doug told her as he swatted her burning bottom. "And I certainly better not hear about reckless driving of any kind. Do I make myself clear?"

She knew he required an answer. She managed an affirmative noise even as the tears covered her face.

Tia froze as she heard the unmistakable sound of Doug taking off his belt. "No," she said, her tears falling faster now. She choked on her voice. "Please, Doug."

The belt came out of the loops, and Tia felt it tap against her unfortunate bottom.

"You're going to remember this, Tia Annalisa," her husband announced. "You know damn well that I will spank you hard if that's what I have to do to keep you safe."

Tia shot forward when the belt smacked her low across both cheeks. The searing pain was immediate and felt unbearable on her already spanked bottom. She let out a sob and lowered her head onto the box in front of her.

Tia continued to heave and cry as Doug finished spanking her with the belt. She could tell by the fire that her bottom was swollen and red.

Doug delivered the last swat with force and put his belt back on while Tia cried. When she was no longer shaking with sobs, he took her shoulders and pulled her up to a standing position.

"You scared me," he said, his voice calmer now. "Don't ever do that again."

"I won't," Tia cried. She buried her face in his chest.

He held her for several minutes allowing her to cry it all out. Tia knew that he'd only been as harsh as she deserved, and she knew that now the slate was clear. She only had to remember to drive carefully from that day on, just as she should have from the very beginning.

After she'd calmed down, Doug took her hand and led her out of the small room. She knew her face was tear-streaked and that her eyes were puffy. She could hardly look Mr. Brand in the eye when they made the couple made their way back into the waiting room.

"Sit down," Doug said to her, indicating the chair where she'd been seated when he first entered the building.

She thought of her sore bottom, still throbbing from her spanking. She decided she'd rather stand. "But Doug, I…"

"Sit," Doug commanded. Apparently he was thinking of her sore bottom as well.

She seated herself on the chair and tried to find a comfortable position. Her bottom hurt and all she wanted was to go home, take a nice bath and climb into bed.

She waited while Doug and Mr. Brand discussed the dim future of her car. Then she jumped to her feet as Doug reached for her hand and told her it was time to go.

She glanced at Mr. Brand. He gave her a smile and a wink. She smiled back and then followed her husband through the front door.

Checking Her Engine

"Gabby!"

Gabby froze, the clean sheet in her hands. She had been changing the sheets on the bed when she'd heard the roar through the open window. It did not sound like the kind of summons she wanted to answer. She knew from experience, however, that it was best to find out what was wrong. She leaned out the window to see Rich in the driveway next to the car. He looked up at her, and she could tell that something had made him mad. She hoped it wasn't her.

Rich wasn't especially tall, but he had a monstrous upper body. His biceps were huge, and his arms were tattooed all the way down. He usually rode his Harley rather than drive the family car.

Gabby was so different from her husband that their friends thought it was very amusing. She was a teacher and could often be found wearing a cardigan with big apples or some other bright object for decoration. She had wild, curly brown hair and freckles. Rich's friends liked to refer to the couple as beauty and the beast.

"Gabby!" he bellowed a second time.

"Be right there," Gabby called. She skipped down the stairs and out the front door of the little farmhouse. The driveway was loose gravel, and it wound its way through a group of trees before meeting the road. The land they lived on had once been a farm. Gabby and Rich both liked the privacy of the wide-open spaces.

Rich waited for Gabby to approach and give him a peck on the cheek. "What's up?"

"How long as this engine light been on?" he asked her, scowling.

Gabby's mouth fell open. She had completely forgotten about the light. She had intended to take the car to the mechanic or at least point it out to Rich, but it had slipped her mind. "I… uh.."

"How long?" he repeated.

"About a month," she admitted. She closed her eyes, waiting for the explosion.

"A month?" Rich looked perplexed. "A month? And you didn't say anything? Are you trying to destroy the car?"

“I kept forgetting,” Gabby told him. She twisted a brown ringlet of hair in her fingers. “I was going to take it to Liam’s shop, but I never got around to it.”

“Girl,” Rich said quietly. He took a step toward her.

Gabby swallowed. With Rich, quiet was trouble. “What are you going to do?”

He took another step, and Gabby stepped backwards away from him. “I am going to take a look under your hood and warm your chassis.”

“Now Rich,” Gabby began, hoping her voice would have a calming effect. “Let’s talk about this.”

Rich shook his head and reached for her. He flipped up her little skirt and wiggled her out of her tights and panties. Then he bent her under his arm, and her feet left the ground.

He swatted her bottom as she kicked in the air and yelled out his name in a vain attempt to stop the assault. As usual, Rich paid no attention to her pleas. Instead he peppered her bottom with sharp slaps until she stopped yelling and started sniffling.

“You will not leave the engine light on,” Rich growled. “Say it.”

"I will not leave the engine light on!" Gabby repeated.

Rich gave her ten hard smacks. "Say it again!"

"I will not leave the engine light on!" she said again.

He finished her spanking with a flurry of hard whaps. When he put her down, she was breathing hard. Her eyes stung with tears, and her face was red from embarrassment and from struggling.

Gabby folded her arms and looked up at Rich. "Are you happy now?" she demanded.

"Yes," Rich told her, a satisfied grin on his face. He reached down between her legs, and she felt her knees grow weak with his touch. She couldn't help that his dominance made her crazy with desire.

"You have a leak," he told her matter-of-factly. "I think I'm going to need to check that out upstairs"

He took her hand and led her back into the house. She scrambled up the stairs, and he was right behind her.

Tucker's Girl

It was an absolutely beautiful spring day. It was the kind of warm a person waited all winter to feel. Amber had the top down on her convertible, and she was relishing the feeling of her long hair blowing in the wind.

She was alone on the old highway as far as she could tell. Most of the traffic was on the new expressway built the past year. It had four lanes of cars in each direction, and it would get any vehicle across the metro area in no time. That's if it wasn't rush hour, of course.

Amber preferred the old two-lane split highway with its neglected roads that sidled up to the woods. There were a few gas stations still open and several churches along the way. Every once in awhile she'd pass an antique store or a knitting shop, but for the most part businesses had relocated to areas that saw more consumers.

She was feeling especially free, like she was on the open road. She loved the way her car responded so easily to the smallest movement of her feet on the pedals. She pushed down on the gas and felt a whoosh of excitement as she sped away from town. She took a corner at a breakneck speed, nearly putting her little car on two wheels. She whooped into the air after the turn. She was feeling like she could fly.

That's when she heard it. Annoyed, she glanced into her rearview mirror. Sure enough, red and blue lights flashed as the police car pulled up behind her. She groaned and pulled her car to the side of the road.

The officer who pulled her over was Jerry Yoder. He'd been a cop since Amber was a teenager. In fact, he'd probably been the one to pull her over when she was sixteen. He'd also been a groomsman when she'd married Tucker five years before. He was an old school police officer. He'd taken Tucker under his wing when Tuck was a rookie cop. The two had been buddies ever since.

"Amber Michelle Johnson O'Reilly," Jerry said as he approached the car. "Just what in the hell do you think you're doing?"

Amber grinned. "You're lookin' good, Jerry."

Jerry had the looks of an attractive, older man. His hair was still dark, but his temples were a sophisticated gray. She also appreciated the way he filled out the uniform.

"Flattery will get you nowhere, babe," Jerry replied. "You know how fast you were going?"

Amber considered the question and then shook her head. "Actually, I don't."

"You were going ninety-two miles per hour, young lady," Jerry told her.

Amber cringed. "I didn't realize."

The police officer shook his head. "I know you didn't realize, girl. You know what the speed limit is on this stretch?"

Again, Amber had no idea.

"It's fifty," Jerry informed her. "You were going forty miles above the speed limit. I could take you in for that."

"I'm sorry, Jer," she said. She made sure to open her brown eyes wide and stick out her chest just a little. Jerry was nearly old enough to be her father, but she figured it couldn't hurt.

Jerry either didn't notice her tricks or didn't respond. He was reaching into his pocket.

Amber scoffed. “You’re not going to write me a ticket?”

It was an unwritten rule on the force that an officer didn’t write tickets to family members of another officer. Everyone knew it, and Amber knew Jerry wasn’t about to break a code like that.

“I am not going to write you a ticket,” Jerry told her. He pulled a cell phone out of his pocket. “I am going to call your husband.”

“Aw Jer,” Amber protested, anxiety rising in her chest. “Don’t do that.”

“That’s my protocol,” Jerry explained. He was searching through his phone for Tucker’s number. “I picked up Christy Larson for underage drinking last week. I called Patrick, and he came on over and whipped her little behind.”

“Christy Larson is sixteen, and Patrick is her father.” Amber argued. “I’m a grown woman.”

“You need to be handled,” Jerry said. “And I figure Tucker is the one to do the handling.”

Amber let her head flop onto the steering wheel. This was not going as she’d hoped.

“Hey Tuck,” Jerry said into his phone. “I got your little woman here... Uh huh…. Uh huh.”

Amber sighed loudly. Jerry winked at her. “Doing ninety-two in a fifty…. Yep, that’s right…. Over here on the old highway… Uh huh… Uh huh… Yep.”

Jerry closed his phone and grinned at Amber. “He’ll be right over.”

Amber shook her head. “Jerry, I could kill you right now.”

“Tucker’s gonna kick your butt, and you deserve it,” Jerry said.

Amber pressed her lips into a sneer. Jerry had it partially right. Her butt was on the line, but it wasn’t going to be kicked. “Don’t you have somewhere to be?”

Jerry’s smile was wide. “I’m keeping my eye on you until Tucker gets here.”

It turned out they didn’t have to wait long. Tucker had been only a few miles away. Amber watched in her rearview as her husband’s cruiser pulled up behind her.

Tucker got out of his car, and he didn’t look happy. He was a big man, tall and muscular. He usually sported a lop-sided smile that Amber found charming. Now his jaw was firm, and his mouth was tight.

He walked swiftly toward the car, glanced at his wife and then looked at Jerry. “Ninety-two?”

The older cop nodded. “That’s right.”

Tucker put his hands on his hips and turned sharp eyes on his wife. Amber felt like she was shrinking under his gaze.

“Ninety-two, Amber?”

“That’s what Jerry says,” Amber answered apologetically.

“And I suppose you weren’t paying enough attention to know if that’s accurate?”

He had her there. She shook her head. “No sir.”

Jerry patted Tucker on the back. “I’ll leave you two alone,” he said. He nodded toward Amber. “You behave yourself, now.”

Amber wanted to flip him the bird, but she didn’t think it would help her situation.

“Out of the car,” Tucker ordered.

“Tuck… can’t we talk about this later?” Amber asked him. She wanted him to have time to cool down, and she wanted time to plan her excuses.

“Get your butt out of the car right now,” Tucker snapped.

Her husband's tone had left no room for argument, and Amber scrambled to obey. She stepped out of the car and had to slide past Tucker, who didn't move an inch.

Amber was wearing a blue tank top, white jeans and strappy sandals. Her brown hair fell over her shoulders in waves. She instinctively took a few steps away from her husband. Tucker looked angry, and she didn't want to tangle with an angry Tucker.

He started in on her immediately. "What is the matter with you, Amber?"

She shrugged and bit her lower lip. "Nothing. I just… I was just having fun. There was no one around."

"Jerry was around."

"Okay, no one but Jerry. It was just such a nice day that I decided to drive a little fast." Amber knew that she was just digging herself into a hole with her words.

"If you want to drive fast I'll get you a NASCAR weekend for your birthday," Tucker said. He was towering over her, and he still looked really mad. "You don't drive fast on public roads."

She nodded. "I know. I won't do it again."

“You certainly won’t,” Tucker said. He took her by the arm and flipped her around. Then he smacked her jeans three times, hard. Amber jumped. Tucker was wearing his thick police officer’s gloves, and they added a heavy thud to an otherwise heavy hand.

“Ow! Tuck! Not here!” she protested.

“You said yourself there’s no one out here,” her husband reminded her. “If anyone does happen to drive by, they’re going to see you getting your little bottom spanked.”

Amber felt a wave of panic. He was going to spank her on the side of the highway? “Tuck, please.”

Tucker was a man of action, and he was through listening. In one motion he undid the fly of Amber’s jeans and slid them to her knees.

She gasped and grabbed the fabric of her pants to pull them back up over her hips. Tucker was fast, though. He snatched her hands away and bent her over the side of her convertible. With his left hand he pinned her hands to her back. With his right hand he began to wallop her red panties. The gloved hand fell rapidly, and Amber was squirming in no time.

Tucker pulled her panties down. Then he reached into her jeans pocket and took out her car keys. He leaned over and turned on the car as Amber waited, her bare bottom stinging.

"What are you doing?" Amber asked.

Tucker didn't answer. He left the car running and returned his attention to his wife.

Amber felt Tucker put a glove on her bare bottom, and she wiggled. He cupped his hand over her cheeks and then moved the glove into her crack. Between the sting and the touching Amber was overcome with sensation.

Amber squeezed her eyes shut as a car drove by them. She didn't want to know whether or not the driver saw her predicament.

After caressing her bottom for about thirty seconds, Tucker got back to business. He began slapping her bare bottom, knocking her pelvis against the side of the running car.

"Ow! Tucker, stop!" Amber demanded. She tried to push herself up, but Tucker held her down.

"You want me to spank you with your bottom facing traffic?" he asked.

Amber shook her head violently. She didn't think he would do that, not to preserve her modesty but because it didn't seem safe. She wasn't interested in finding out, though.

Tucker spanked her hard, each whack echoing off the trees. By the time he was finished, she was crying. He pulled her up off the car and lifted her into his arms.

"Tuck? What are you doing? Tuck?" she asked him. Her bottom was blazing, and she just wanted to go home.

Tucker carried her to the front of the car and deposited her bare bottom on the hood.

"Ow!" Amber screamed, wiggling herself silly. Tucker held her down until she stopped struggling. The hood of the car was warm, and it burned her already sore, stinging bottom. On top of that, she was sitting on a car on the side of the highway in broad daylight with her pants down.

She looked into Tucker's eyes and started to cry. He took the opportunity to scold her.

"No speeding. You got that?"

"Yes sir," she said, nodding. "Please, Tuck."

"Does your bottom hurt?"

"You know it does," she wailed.

"You created this heat with your reckless driving. I'm going to make sure it sticks," Tucker said. "I bet the heat from this car is stinging your little rear."

She nodded again. "Let me up."

"You're in time-out," he told her with a joyful grin. "I believe it's one minute for each year of your age. That's twenty-six minutes."

Amber groaned. She did not want to sit bare-bottomed on the warm car for twenty-six minutes. She was sure her bottom would be scorched. She started to cry harder. Tucker put pressures on her shoulder so that her bottom was squashed into the hood of the car.

"Lucky for you, I have to get back to work," he told her. He lifted her up off the hood and gave her a quick, hard spanking that left her sobbing. Then he pulled up her pants and panties.

"You're going to get in that car, and you're going to drive yourself home slowly," he told her evenly.

She nodded, and he kissed her on the nose. She climbed into the car and he watched as she put on her seatbelt. Her bottom was still flaming, but she had managed to stop crying.

“Behave yourself,” he said sternly before turning back to his cruiser.

Amber pulled back onto the highway and headed toward home. In her rearview mirror she saw Tucker driving back to his duties as a police officer. She watched him until he was out of sight.

A Note From Jennie…

I hope you've enjoyed reading these short stories as much as I've enjoyed writing them!

I do not necessarily endorse or condone my characters' opinions or actions, but I do find them exceptionally hot.

If you'd like to get to know me better I hope you will take a look at my blog www.ageplaystories.blogspot.com

Happy spankings.

Jennie

www.ingramcontent.com/pod-product-compliance
Ingram Content Group UK Ltd.
Pitfield, Milton Keynes, MK11 3LW, UK
UKHW041839200726
13854UKWH00003BA/1213

9 780557 241231